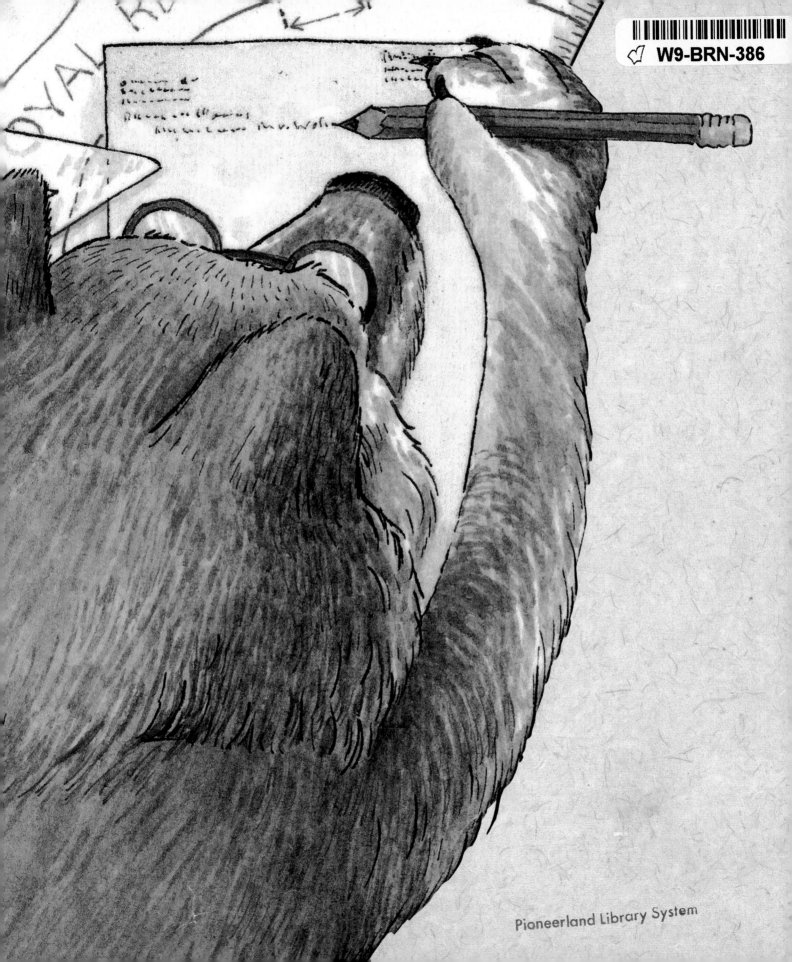

Yours Truly, Goldilocks

by

ALMA FLOR ADA

illustrated by

LESLIE TRYON

ATHENEUM BOOKS *for* YOUNG READERS

Para Camilita porque te quiero mucho
and to Jonathan Lanman, best of editors
—A. F. A.

For dear J. B. O.
—L. T.

✶

Atheneum Books for Young Readers
An imprint of Simon & Schuster Children's Publishing Division
1230 Avenue of the Americas
New York, New York 10020

Text copyright © 1998 by Alma Flor Ada
Illustrations copyright © 1998 by Leslie Tryon

Book design by Michael Nelson
The illustrations in this book are rendered in pen-and-ink with watercolor.

First Edition
Printed in the United States of America
10 9 8 7 6 5 4 3 2 1

Library of Congress Cataloging-in-Publication Data
Ada, Alma Flor.
Yours truly, Goldilocks / by Alma Flor Ada ; illustrated by Leslie Tryon.—1st ed.
p. cm.
Summary: Presents the correspondence of Goldilocks, the Three Pigs, Baby Bear, Peter Rabbit,
and Little Red Riding Hood as they plan to attend a house warming party for the pigs and avoid the evil wolves in the forest.
ISBN 0-689-81608-1
[1. Characters in literature—Fiction. 2. Letters—Fiction.] I. Tryon, Leslie, ill. II. Title.
PZ7.A1857Yo 1998
[E]—dc21
97-10696

Brick House
Woodsy Woods
April 7

Goldilocks McGregor
McGregor's Farm
Veggie Lane

Dear Goldilocks,

Thank you, thank you, thank you! The three of us had a great time at your birthday party.

It was a wonderful, wonderful, wonderful party. That is, all three of us think it was wonderful.

As you know, we have had a terrible time building our houses. Now that we are sure that no wolf can blow down our new house, no matter how hard he huffs and puffs, we would like to finally have a house warming party on April twenty-ninth. We would be very happy if you were our special guest. We are also sending invitations to Baby Bear, Little Red Riding Hood, and Peter Rabbit. We look forward to a wonderful day.

Love, love, love, your three friends,

Pig One, Pig Two, and Pig Three

Cottage in the Woods
Hidden Forest
April 9

Little Red Riding Hood
Cardinal Cottage
Riding Lane

Dearest Granddaughter,

You have such a wonderful imagination! Just to think . . . a birthday party with bears, rabbits, and pigs. Well, well, I imagine you and Goldilocks must have had fun with your stuffed animals.

Goldilocks sounds like a very nice girl. I have known the McGregor family for a long time. Years ago when I lived on Riding Lane, I used to buy all my vegetables from them. Mr. McGregor is a stern man but a wonderful gardener.

Give a kiss to your mother for me. I hope you can come to see me again soon. I'll be here all day on the twelfth. Why not then? But you must keep your promise to stay on the trail this time. That encounter with the wolf was certainly not imaginary.

Love,

Grandma

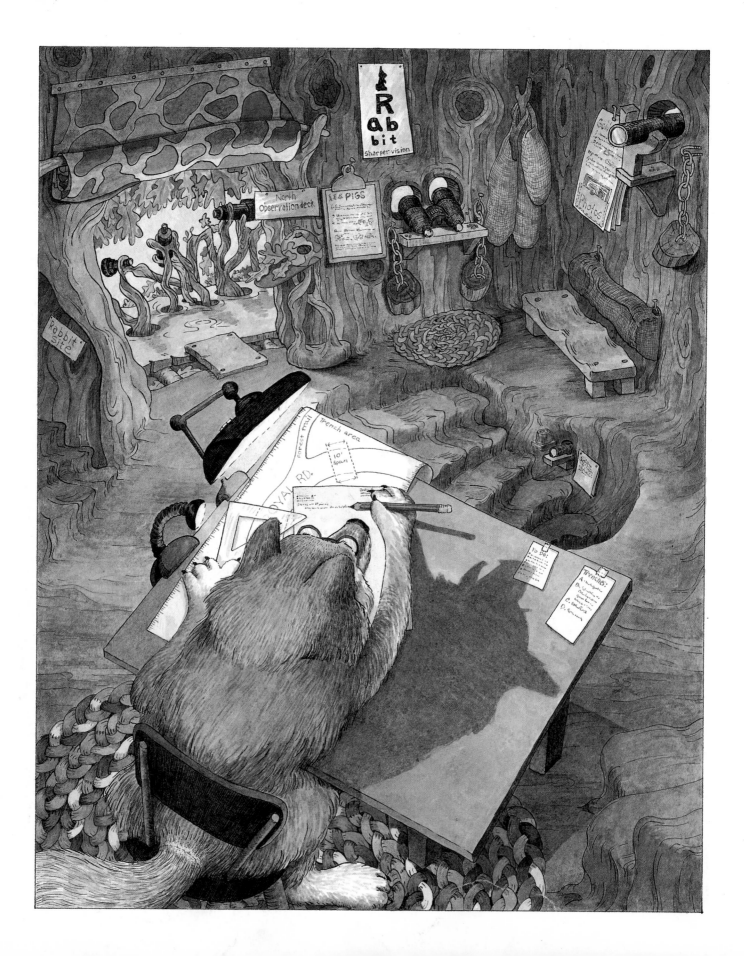

Wolfy Lupus
Wolf Lane
Oakshire

Dear Cousin Wolfy,

After my humiliation at their hands, my continued surveillance of the porcine trio and their friends has finally proven useful.

I have been led to believe that there will be a gathering at their house on the twenty-ninth of April for a house warming party. This means that a delicious bunch of morsels—that is, guests—will be attending and I have a stupendous plan to ensure that not all of them will return home.

A deep trench on Royal Road after the fork will force them to take Forest Trail. It will not be difficult for us to ambush them there.

After their party at that stubborn brick house, we will show them a true party in my majestic tower. What do you think?

Why don't you come to stay on the twenty-seventh? That will give us ample time for the necessary preparations.

Affectionately,

Fer O'Cious

Cardinal Cottage
Riding Lane
April 10

Goldilocks McGregor
McGregor's Farm
Veggie Lane

Dearest Goldilocks,

Have you received an invitation from the three Pigs for their house warming party? After all the fun we had at your birthday it will be wonderful to all get together again. You certainly have interesting friends.

I wrote a long letter to my grandmother telling her all about your birthday party, and she doesn't believe it's true that Peter Rabbit, Baby Bear, and the three Pigs were there.

When I visit her the day after tomorrow I will take the invitation to the house warming party and tell her all about it in person, and she will see it is true.

Do you want to go together to the Pigs' party? My mother says it is okay if you want to come the day before and spend the night. And she will make us some of her special gingerbread cookies.

Your good friend,

LITTLE RED RIDING HOOD

McGregor's Farm
Veggie Lane
April 12

Little Red Riding Hood
Cardinal Cottage
Riding Lane

Dear Little Red Riding Hood,

Yes, I did receive the invitation and I would love to spend the night at your house and go together to the house warming party. Do you have any idea what one does at a house warming party? I know the Pigs have been trying to have one for a long time. Do you think we bring blankets to warm the house?

Baby Bear would like for us to go play hide-and-seek a week from Sunday. His cousins Teddy and Osito are visiting. Do you want to go? I love houses in the forest, don't you?

Be careful on your visit to your grandmother. My father says there definitely still are wolves around.

I have to write to the Pigs and Baby Bear, and I still need to water three rows of vegetables, so I must go now.

Your busy friend,

Goldilocks

Wolf Lane
Oakshire
April 13

Fer O'Cious
Majestic Tower
Hidden Lane
Wooden Heights

Dear Cousin Fer,

You are definitely right about the forthcoming event on April twenty-ninth. Yesterday, as I was trailing that appetizing-looking creature in red, she seemed to have gotten scared somehow. As she ran into her grandmother's house, she dropped an invitation on the path. Sure enough, those pigs of yours are inviting everyone to a house warming party. I am enclosing the foolish card for your perusal.

I found any mention to warming in their house somewhat distasteful, their description of their abode pretentious, and their reference to us rather offensive.

There is no question that I will join you in your efforts. I like your plan and I will be there on the twenty-seventh with ready paws and sharpened teeth!

Your affectionate cousin,

Wolfy

McGregor's Farm
Veggie Lane
April 13

Baby Bear
Bear House in the Woods
Hidden Meadow

Dear Baby Bear,

Your letter was very nice. I have always loved getting letters. Although right now I am getting so many, I can't find enough time to answer back. And my father is always after me to go water the vegetables.

I don't mind too much watering the lettuces and the carrots. They grow close to the well and I don't have to carry the watering can that far. But the spinach and the peas are much farther away and that full can gets heavy. I can't understand how anyone likes to eat that green stuff anyway.

I would love to go to your house to play hide-and-seek a week from Sunday and meet your cousins Teddy and Osito. I have already asked Little Red Riding Hood to come also.

Your very good and busy friend,

Goldilocks

McGregor's Farm
Veggie Lane
April 15

Pig One, Pig Two, and Pig Three
Brick House
Woodsy Woods

Dear Pig One, Pig Two, and Pig Three,

A house warming party sounds like a terrific idea! I love parties, but I have never been to a house warming one yet. How do we warm the house? Do you want us to bring blankets?

Little Bear would like to play hide-and-seek. Would you like to come to his house a week from today? His cousins Teddy and Osito will be there also.

Have you seen or heard from Peter Rabbit? I haven't heard anything from him, except that the one carrot I leave each night outside the hedge is always gone the next morning. Do you know if he is alright? Things are a lot quieter in my house since my father doesn't complain anymore about stolen vegetables, but I miss Peter! If you come to the Bears' house, please bring him along!

Your friend,

Goldilocks

Goldilocks McGregor

McGregor's Farm

Veggie Lane

Dear Goldilocks,

My friends the Pigs came by to see me yesterday, after you all played hide-and-seek at the Bears'. Sorry I couldn't be there.

They told me you were worried about me and I am sorry I have not written before. You see, I have been in bed now for almost three weeks with measles.

Your carrots have been wonderful. Flopsy, Mopsy, and Cotton-tail have been picking them up every morning at dawn. They did not get measles this time because they all had it last year. My mother has been feeding us carrot soup, carrot salad, and carrot cake. I love carrots! She has also been feeding me gallons of chamomile tea. You know my mother loves chamomile tea!

Now that the measles are all gone I will be able to go to the Pigs' party Sunday. See you there!

Thanks again for the carrots!

Your very dearest friend,

Peter Rabbit

P. S. The Pigs convinced my mother to allow Flopsy, Mopsy, and Cotton-tail to come to their party. They are dying to meet you!

Rabbit's Burrow
Hollow Oak
May 1

Mrs. Mother Bear
Bear House in the Woods
Hidden Meadow

Dear Mrs. Bear,

I wanted my mother to help me write you a letter, but she says that if I can get into trouble all by myself, I should be able to write this letter all by myself.

The first thing I want to say to you is THANK YOU VERY MUCH! Thank you for saving me from those two terrible wolves.

As you know, it is usually not very easy for a wolf to catch a rabbit. And I could race those two and win easily anytime. But I was talking to Goldilocks about the party and didn't even see them coming. Before I knew it I was inside that ugly sack. I thought it was the end of all of us.

They tell me you were terrific, and I wish I could have helped you instead of being inside that smelly sack. Thank you again for saving my life.

Gratefully yours,

Peter Rabbit
P. S. Although my mother wanted me to write the letter she is very thankful too. And it wouldn't surprise me at all if she were planning something special to thank you.

Speedy Raccoon, Furrier
Forest Drive
Hidden Forest

Dear Mr. Raccoon:

My cousin Mr. Wolfy Lupus and I are in great need of your services again. Both of us have been the unfortunate victims at the paws of an angry mother bear.

Since we are both bedridden, would you be able to make a house call to take the necessary measurements?

I will be needing a new tail. I trust you will be able to provide one of an elegant deep gray color to match the rest of my beautiful fur. My cousin will require some large patches on the back as well as a supplementary ear.

To imagine that a bear would go to such lengths to defend a couple of little girls and some silly rabbits! We certainly did not mean to bother her bear cub at all.

We look forward to hearing from you at your earliest convenience since we would like to change our sorrowful state.

Sincerely,

Fer O'Cious

McGregor's Farm
Veggie Lane
May 1

Pig One, Pig Two, and Pig Three
Brick House
Woodsy Woods

Dear Pig One, Pig Two, and Pig Three,

Your house warming party was truly spectacular. I didn't know what a house warming party was all about before it started. It was great to realize that a house is warmed with friends, fun, and laughter.

As I am sure you know by now, several of us had a horrific experience on our way home after the party. It was very scary!

Little Red Riding Hood and I have been thinking we should all get together to plan how to thank Mother Bear for saving our lives and how to make sure those ugly wolves cannot hurt us.

Please begin thinking of wonderful ideas. When we decide a time and place to meet, we will let you know.

Enjoy your brick house!

Yours Truly,
Goldilocks